W9-BKK-523
CREATED BY
ROBERT KIRKMAN &
LORENZO DE FELICI

ROBERT KIRKMAN
WRITER/CREATOR

LORENZO DE FELICI
ARTIST/CREATOR

ANNALISA LEONI
COLORIST

RUS WOOTON
LETTERER

KATE CAUDILL
ASSISTANT EDITOR

SEAN MACKIEWICZ
EDITOR

LORENZO DE FELICI
COVER

ANDRES JUAREZ
LOGO & PRODUCTION DESIGN

CARINA TAYLOR
PRODUCTION

SKYBOUND

Foreign Rights Inquiries: ag@sequentialrights.com
Other Licensing Inquiries: contact@skybound.com

WWW.SKYBOUND.COM

WWW.IMAGECOMICS.COM

image

OBLIVION SONG VOLUME THREE. First Printing. Published by Image Comics, Inc. Office of publication: 2701 NW Vaughn St., Ste. 780, Portland, OR 97210. Printed in the U.S.A. For information regarding the CPSIA on this printed material call: 203-595-3636. ISBN: 978-1-5343-1326-2

CHAPTER THREE

THIS EVERYTHING FOR TODAY'S SHIPMENT?

THAT'S EVERYTHING THAT WAS READY TO HARVEST. WE'RE BRINGING BACK A FULL LOAD.
GREAT NEWS. EVERYONE READY?
ALL SET.
CARGO IS AWAY.
BEEP BEEP!
FWAAASH!
OKAY, NOW FOR--
OH, GOD--!

I'LL DRAW ITS ATTENTION-- GET OUT OF HERE!
HURRY!
OKAY. OKAY.
TEK

THREE YEA
PETERIA
EVERYONE BACK OKAY?
THANKS TO YOU, YEAH. THAT WAS AMAZING. THAT THING COULD HAVE KILLED YOU.
JUST DOING MY JOB, CYNTHIA.

RS LATER
OH, CRAP-- QUICK, HELP ME WITH THE SAMPLES.
WHAT IS IT--
OH.
HEY!
YOU THINK I DIDN'T SEE THAT?! YOU CAN'T AVOID ME--

--MARCO!
AVOID YOU? DON'T BE CRAZY, DIRECTOR WARD. I'D NEVER DO THAT. I JUST WANTED TO HELP GET THESE SAMPLES LOADED UP AS SOON AS POSSIBLE.
WHAT CAN I DO FOR YOU?
YOU MAY NOT WORK DIRECTLY FOR ME, BUT YOU ARE SUBJECT TO MY OVERSIGHT--AND IF YOU'RE NOT GOING TO FILL OUT YOUR REPORTS IN FULL, THERE AIN'T A WHOLE HELL OF A LOT FOR ME TO OVERSEE.
UNDERSTAND?
I'M SORRY, SIR-- WE'VE JUST BEEN SO BUSY LATELY...
BRIDGET & DUNCAN FREEMAN FOUNDATION

...FUNDING FROM BOTH GOVERNMENT AND PRIVATE SOURCES. THESE RESOURCES HAVE ALLOWED US TO EXPAND RAPIDLY OVER THE LAST TWO YEARS.
THESE NEW STRAINS OF ANTIBIOTICS HAVE CHANGED MODERN MEDICINE. OUR NEW VACCINES HAVE ALREADY RID THE WORLD OF MALARIA, CHOLERA, AND SO MANY OTHER ILLNESSES. WE ARE RAPIDLY APPROACHING CURES FOR MANY MORE THAT WERE DEADLY A MATTER OF MONTHS AGO--OUR WORK HAS ALREADY SAVED COUNTLESS LIVES.
BRIDGET & DUNCAN FREEMAN FOUNDATION
OBLIVION HAS PROVEN ITSELF TO BE AN ABUNDANT RESOURCE THAT SHOULD BE FURTHER EXPLORED AND STUDIED.
THAT IS WHY THIS IS NOT A TIME FOR CELEBRATION OF WHAT WE HAVE ACCOMPLISHED... IT IS TIME TO REDOUBLE OUR EFFORTS BECAUSE WE KNOW THAT WE ARE ON THE CUSP OF ACCOMPLISHING SO MUCH MORE.
WITH YOUR HELP, THE BRIDGET AND DUNCAN FREEMAN FOUNDATION CAN CONTINUE TO MAKE THE WORLD A BETTER PLACE.

THAT WENT WELL.
IT DID.
YOU'RE CARRYING ME AS ALWAYS.
YOU KNOW THAT'S NOT TRUE.
BABY, YOU WERE GREAT.
OH MY GOD, I WAS SO NERVOUS FOR YOU. I DON'T KNOW HOW YOU DO THAT.

HOLY CRAP, NATHAN, THIS TOOTHBRUSH WORKS BETTER THAN IT DID BEFORE IT BROKE. YOU'RE A MIRACLE WORKER.
ANY TIME, DON. IT WAS A VERY SIMPLE MECHANISM.
COLE!
WARDEN WANTS TO SEE YOU.
WHAT IS IT, HE GETTING LONELY?
JUST START WALKING.

HOW ARE BONNIE AND THE KIDS?
MY OLDEST NEEDS BRACES, SO YOU'LL BE SEEING ME PULL A LOT OF OVERTIME.
MY BOOK LIGHT BROKE AGAIN. CAN YOU TAKE A LOOK AT IT?
HAPPY TO, SAM.
ANY CLUE WHAT THIS IS ABOUT?
COULDN'T TELL YOU IF I KNEW, MAN. SORRY.

DIRECTOR WARD? THIS CAN'T BE GOOD.
TAKE A SEAT, NATHAN. WE'RE GOING TO HAVE US A LITTLE CHAT.
THE RESULTS OF THE INQUIRY HAVE BEEN INCONCLUSIVE... AGAIN. THOUGHT YOU SHOULD BE THE FIRST TO KNOW.
WE'VE HAD ALL OF OUR TOP SCIENTISTS RUNNING THE NUMBERS FOR NEARLY TWO YEARS NOW, AND THE RESULTS KEEP COMING BACK THE SAME.
NO MATTER HOW THEY SLICE IT, THERE SIMPLY WASN'T ENOUGH POWER FOR YOUR DEVICE TO HAVE HAD THE RANGE IT HAD. THEY'RE SAYING SOMETHING FROM THE OTHER SIDE MUST HAVE BOOSTED IT.
FROM EVERYTHING I'VE ALWAYS SEEN IN OBLIVION, IT'S A PRIMITIVE WORLD...
...BUT MAYBE.
BOTTOM LINE, IT'S CALLING INTO QUESTION JUST HOW RESPONSIBLE YOU WERE FOR THE TRANSFERENCE...

DOCUMENTS
VISITOR
DIRECTOR WARD?
I'M SORRY, HEATHER, BUT YOU'RE NOT GOING TO BE ALLOWED TO VISIT NATHAN TODAY...

...BECAUSE YOU'LL BE TAKING HIM HOME.
I'D HAVE MET YOU IN THE PARKING LOT, BUT I HAD TO FIX A BOOK LIGHT, AND I THOUGHT THAT THIS WOULD BE MORE **DRAMATIC.**
OH MY GOD!

COME ON, JAILBIRD, LET'S GET YOU HOME.
OKAY... JAILBIRD.
HEY! I ONLY DID ONE YEAR.
STILL COUNTS.

YOU HEAR THAT?
NO, DANE. YOU HEAR SOMETHING?
PROBABLY NOTHING.
ALL SET.
ALRIGHT, PEOPLE, LET'S GET THIS WATER HOME!

ALL CLEAR.
JEEZ, YOU REALLY DO THIS TWICE A WEEK?
SOMETIMES THREE, ROOKIE. IT'S GOOD TO GET OUT OF CAMP FROM TIME TO TIME.
DON'T FEEL BAD. DANE IS THE ONLY ONE WHO ENJOYS THIS.
OH, COME ON, THESE GUYS CLEARLY LOVE IT, TOO!

HEEELP!
HEEEELP!
WHERE IS IT COMING FROM?
I CAN'T TELL!
HEELP ME!
STAY HERE WITH THE MULES!
DEREK, JILL-- YOU'RE WITH ME!

HELP ME, PLEEAAAASE!
THIS WAY!
I'M SCARED!

I AM A SCAARED HUUMAAAN WHO NEEEDS HELP.

WHAT IS THAT?!
RUN!
HELP MEEE.
DO NOT RUN.

OH, GOD!
WHAT?!
WHAT WAS IT?!
WE HAVE TO GET OUT OF HERE!

IT'S CHASING ME--WE HAVE TO HURRY!
WHAT'S CHASING YOU?
OH MY GOD!
JUST LEAVE IT!

DANE!
JUST KEEP GOING!
P-KOW!

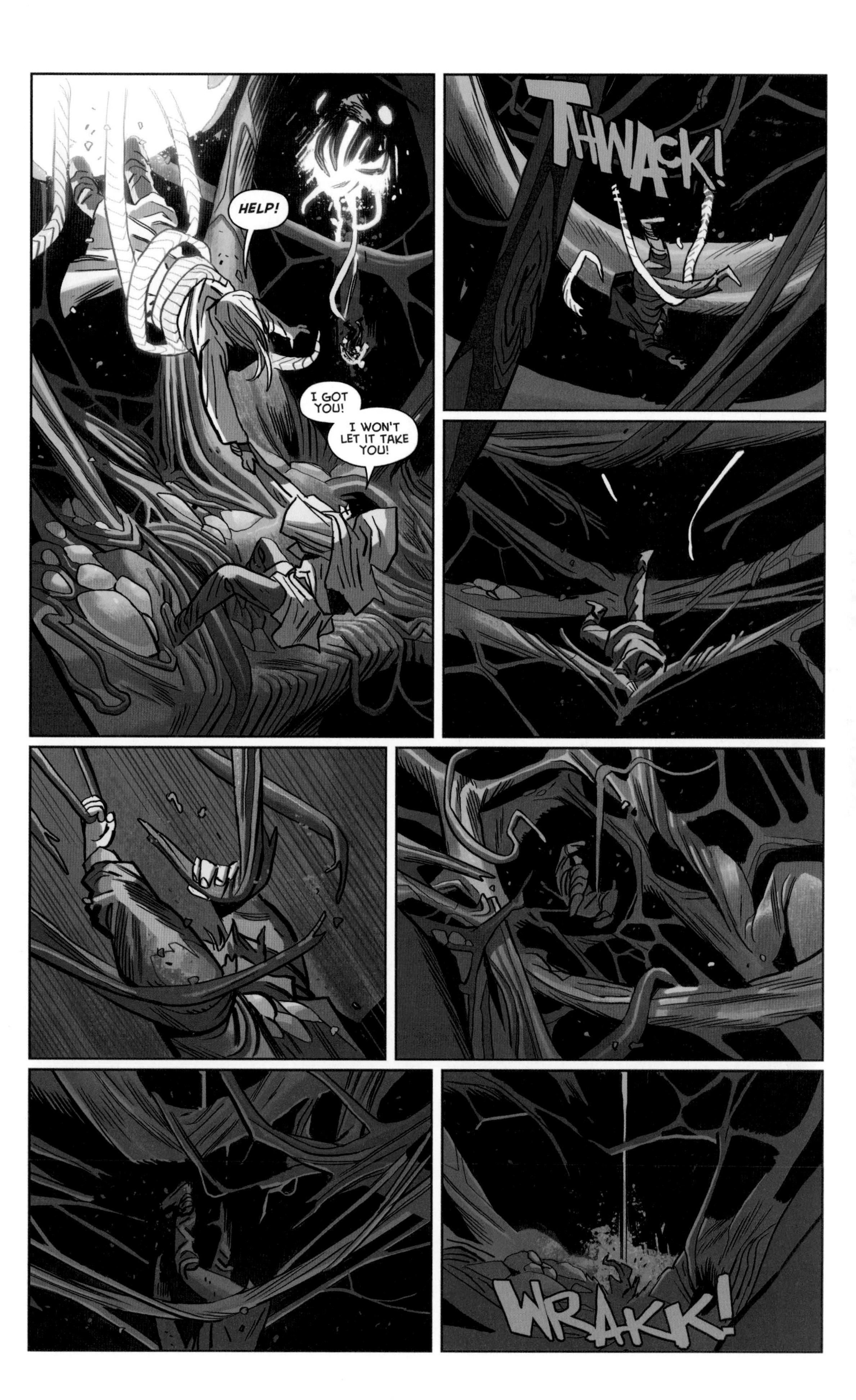
HELP!
I GOT YOU!
I WON'T LET IT TAKE YOU!
THWACK!
WRAKK!

UNGH..
IT HAS ME!
OH, GOD! OH, GOD!
OH--!

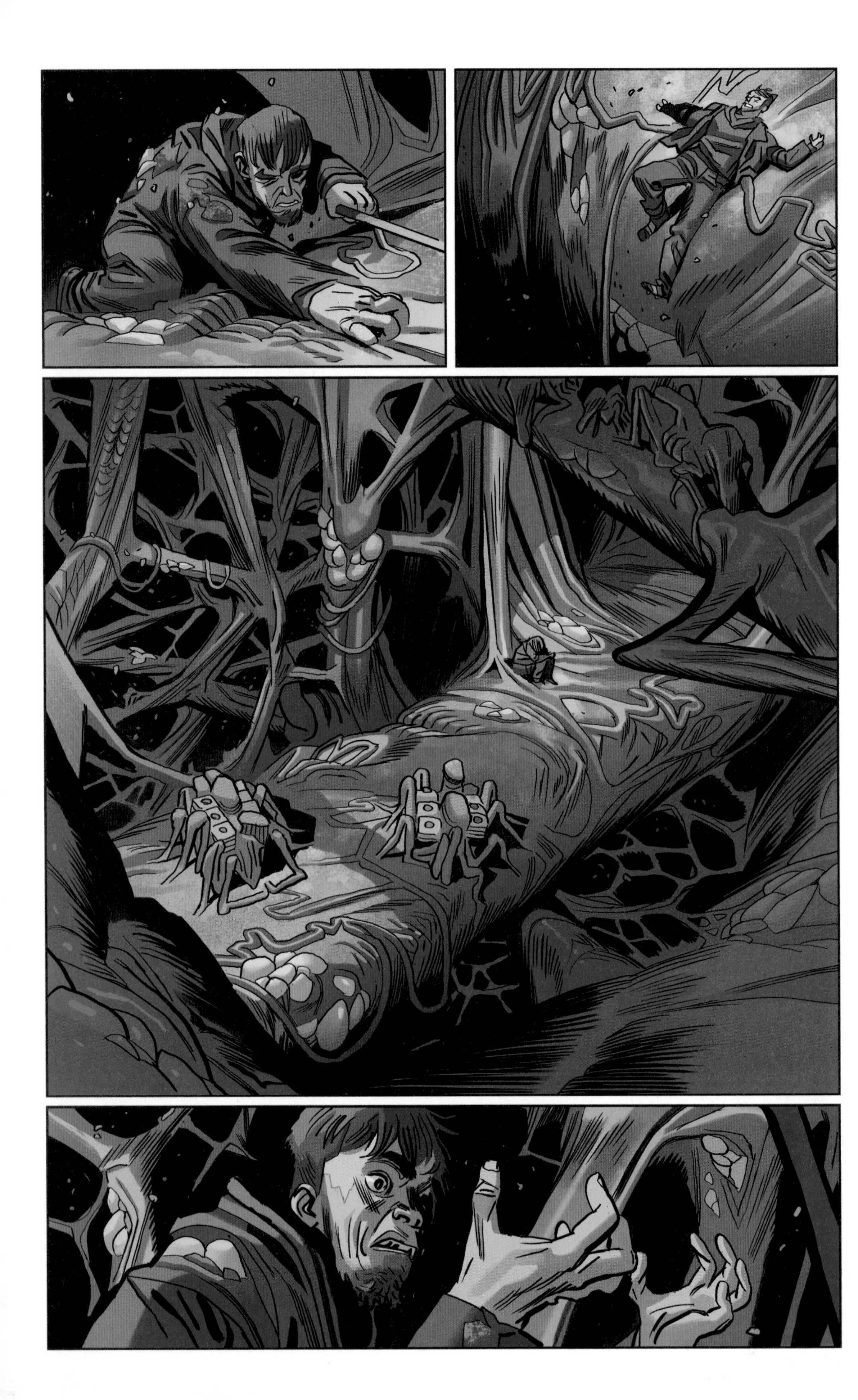

HOW ARE YOU STILL ASLEEP?
WAKE UP, I MADE YOU BREAKFAST.
SORRY, I'M USED TO BEING WOKEN UP...
WELL, HURRY UP AND GET READY. WE'RE GOING TO NEED TO LEAVE SOON IF WE'RE GOING TO BE ON TIME.
WHERE ARE WE GOING?
YOU'LL SEE.

OH NO. WHAT'S THIS?
OH, STOP. YOU'LL LIKE IT.
WELCOME HOME NATHAN
OH...

MARCO?! THIS IS YOUR PLACE?
YOUR OLD JOB PAYS A HELL OF A LOT BETTER NOW.
NEW MANAGEMENT IS PRETTY GREAT.
WELCOME BACK, NATHAN.
IT'S GOOD TO BE BACK, BRIDGET.
HI, BENJAMIN.
NICE TO BE ABLE TO TALK TO YOU WITHOUT THE GLASS BETWEEN US.
HA!
YOU'RE TELLING ME.
DUNCAN, HEY. GOOD TO FINALLY SEE YOU.
I'M VERY SORRY, NATHAN.
I HAVE NO EXCUSE FOR NOT VISITING YOU. THERE WAS SO MUCH GOING ON, THINGS NEVER SEEMED TO QUIET DOWN... I'M IN A MUCH BETTER PLACE NOW.
IT WOULD'VE BEEN NICE TO HEAR FROM YOU, BUT DON'T WORRY ABOUT IT.
I'M JUST HAPPY TO SEE YOU NOW.
THANKS, MAN.

OKAY, SPILL IT. I'M DYING TO KNOW HOW GOOD I LOOK OUTSIDE OF THE SURVIVAL GEAR YOU LAST SAW ME IN.
MARIA!
I HAD HEARD YOU WERE LIVING ON THIS SIDE, IT'S GREAT TO SEE YOU.
YOU LOOK GREAT.
NICELY DONE, ADDING THAT IN AT THE END.
YOU HEAR ANYTHING FROM MY BROTHER? HOW'S HE DOING?
HE'S VERY HAPPY. HE AND LUCY ARE DOING WELL. I HEAR THE CAMP IS THRIVING, EXPANDING, ALL THAT GOOD STUFF.
MARCO HELPS ME EXCHANGE LETTERS WITH ED FROM TIME TO TIME.
WHAT ABOUT YOUR SON? HOW IS HE ADJUSTING TO LIFE HERE?
HE LIVED MOST OF HIS LIFE IN OBLIVION. I WOULD LOVE TO SIT DOWN AND TALK TO HIM SOMETIME.
MATEO? IT'S BEEN A BIT OF AN ADJUSTMENT FOR HIM, BUT HE'S GETTING USED TO IT.
THE HARDEST PART IS THAT HE DOESN'T REALLY RELATE TO OTHER KIDS... IT'S LIKE HE DESPISES THEM FOR HOW EASY THEIR LIVES ARE...
AND HOW THEY DON'T APPRECIATE IT.

YEAH, I CAN SEE HOW THAT WOULD BE FRUSTRATING.
IT'S BEEN DIFFICULT, BUT WORTH IT. I UNDERSTAND ED, LIFE CAN BE **HARDER** HERE...
BUT IT'S A WHOLE HELL OF A LOT EASIER IN A LOT OF IMPORTANT WAYS.
I'VE GOT A LOT OF ACCLIMATING TO DO MYSELF. LIFE ON THE OUTSIDE... IT'S BEEN A WHILE. GOTTA GET USED TO FIXING THINGS INSTEAD OF BREAKING THEM.
I'VE BROKEN ENOUGH THINGS... LIVES.
THERE'S A **SCAR** ON THIS WORLD, AND I PUT IT THERE.
THAT'S **BULLSHIT!**

YOU WERE PART OF A TEAM. AT WORST, YOU'RE PARTIALLY RESPONSIBLE FOR AN ACCIDENT.
PEOPLE SEE THAT NOW. BLAMING YOU FOR WHAT HAPPENED IS WRONG.
YOU BLAMING YOURSELF IS *WORSE.*
IF YOU'RE GOING TO BEAT YOURSELF UP OVER THE BAD, THEN YOU HAVE TO TAKE CREDIT FOR THE GOOD.
YOU GAVE THIS WORLD A SCAR, SURE, AND IT'S STRONGER FOR IT.
WITHOUT THAT SCAR, OUR FOUNDATION DOESN'T GET FORMED, OUR WORK DOESN'T GET DONE, THE CURES AND TREATMENTS WE'VE DISCOVERED DON'T HAPPEN.
IN THE LAST YEAR ALONE... TWO-HUNDRED AND THIRTY-FIVE THOUSAND, SIX-HUNDRED AND THIRTY-TWO LIVES... THAT'S HOW MANY HAVE BEEN SAVED BY MEDICINE AND PROCEDURES THAT WERE DISCOVERED BY YOUR *ACCIDENT.*
THAT'S GOING TO GROW *EXPONENTIALLY,* YEAR AFTER YEAR.
YOU MAY BE INDIRECTLY SAVING MORE LIVES THAN ANYONE IN THE HISTORY OF THE WORLD.
KEEP IN MIND, WE ACCOMPLISHED THAT *WITHOUT* FUNDING. NOW WE HAVE MORE MONEY AND RESOURCES THAN WE KNOW WHAT TO DO WITH.
IT'S TRUE.
SO REALLY, THERE'S NO TELLING WHERE WE COULD TAKE THIS.

THANKS, GUYS...
THIS REALLY MEANS A LOT.

HAVE A GOOD TIME?
YEAH.
YOU HARDLY SAID A WORD AFTER EVERYONE'S BIG PEP TALK.
YEAH... THAT...
THAT **HELPED**.
BEING OUT... ALL THE EYES ON ME... I CAN'T HELP BUT WONDER WHAT PEOPLE THINK ABOUT ME. I CAN ONLY IMAGINE WHAT THEY THINK ABOUT WHAT I DID AND HOW IT MAY HAVE HURT THEM OR SOMEONE THEY LOVED.
NOW THAT EVERYONE KNOWS THE TRUTH ABOUT WHAT HAPPENED... IT REALLY WEARS ON ME.

THE TRUTH IS, I FEEL NAKED AND EXPOSED. IT'S BEEN HARD FOR ME TO BE COMFORTABLE IN MY OWN SKIN. SO HEARING IT ALL LAID OUT LIKE THAT... THE POSITIVE ASPECTS OF WHAT HAPPENED...
I REALLY APPRECIATE IT... HELPS ME GET OUT OF MY OWN HEAD.
BUT STILL... THE MORE TIME I SPEND OUT...
IT JUST MAKES ME REALIZE MORE AND MORE HOW MUCH I WANT TO GO BACK.
TO PRISON?
NO...
OBLIVION.

YOU GOING TO STAND OUT HERE ALL DAY?
I COULD USE YOUR HELP. THIS GUY'S BEING A BIT OF A HANDFUL TODAY.
GIVING MOMMY TROUBLE, ARE YOU?
HE'S AN ANGEL NOW, BUT I THINK HE'S JUST TRYING TO MAKE ME LOOK CRAZY. HE'S BEEN SCREAMING ALL MORNING.

I'M SORRY, IT'S JUST--THEY SHOULD HAVE BEEN BACK BY NOW, FOR SURE.
IT'S A ROUTINE WATER RUN. THEY'RE OUT THERE EVERY OTHER DAY. I'M SURE THEY'RE FINE.
DANE KNOWS WHAT HE'S DOING.
WHAT THE--?!

DANE?!
ED-- OH, GOD!
WHAT HAPPENED?!
WHERE ARE THE REST?!
THEY'RE GONE!
THE FACELESS MEN--
THEY'RE REAL!

THE FACELESS MEN ARE...
REAL.
DANE!
DANE!
IS HE--
HE'S BREATHING, HE'S--
WHAT HAPPENED?!
WHERE ARE THE REST OF HIS CREW?!

GET HIM TO THE INFIRMARY!
HURRY!
GET THESE MULES UNLOADED AND STABLED BEFORE WE LOSE THEM!
YES, SIR!
HE WAS TALKING ABOUT FACELESS MEN--WHAT HAPPENED TO HIM OUT THERE?
DID HE LOSE HIS MIND?
FOR OUR SAKE, WE BETTER HOPE HE DID.

SORRY, I JUST WANTED TO *SEE* IT.
IT'S OKAY, I UNDERSTAND.

IT'S JUST BEEN SO LONG. I FELT LIKE I HAD TO LAY EYES ON IT... MAKE SURE IT'S STILL HERE.
I KNOW THAT SOUNDS STUPID.
IT DOESN'T. IT'S OKAY.
YOU WERE AWAY FOR A LONG TIME, NATHAN. I UNDERSTAND. WHATEVER IT TAKES TO GET YOU BACK UP TO SPEED...
I'M HERE FOR YOU.
ALL THESE NAMES, JESUS--
CAN YOU BELIEVE I USED TO TELL MYSELF I WOULD EVENTUALLY CROSS THEM ALL OUT?
THIS PLACE, I'VE ALWAYS HATED IT.
IT WAS A PAINFUL REMINDER OF WHAT I DID...
NOW IT MARKS THE PRICE WE PAID FOR ALL THE GOOD BRIDGET AND DUNCAN ARE DOING.
I WONDER IF NOW THEY HATE IT AS MUCH AS I DID.

OH, GOD. ALL THESE PEOPLE...
IT WAS A *MISTAKE.*
WHAT KIND OF PERSON WOULD I BE IF *THAT* MADE IT *OKAY?*
COME ON, WE SHOULD HURRY.
THEY'RE PROBABLY WAITING...

WOW.
WELL, WHAT DO YOU THINK?
I LOVE WHAT YOU'VE DONE WITH THE PLACE.
YEAH, WE'VE BEEN DOING A LOT OF EXPANDING LATELY.
I BARELY KNOW HALF THESE PEOPLE'S NAMES.
IT'S ALL VERY IMPRESSIVE, BRIDGET.

SOME ANALYSIS IS DONE ON SITE, BUT WE HAVE BETTER EQUIPPED FACILITIES IN THE CITY.
THAT'S WHERE **DUNCAN** SPENDS MOST OF HIS TIME... BETTER AIR CONDITIONING.
WE'RE TRYING TO FIGURE OUT A WAY TO GROW SPORES **HERE** IN **THIS** DIMENSION.
LESS DANGEROUS TRIPS SO WE CAN PRODUCE MORE OF THE VALUABLE PLANT LIFE ON **THIS** SIDE.
WE HAVE MULTIPLE TEAMS WORKING NOW, SO NO ONE HAS TO SPEND AS MUCH TIME OVER THERE AS YOU DID.
THEY WORK IN TIGHTLY SCHEDULED THREE-HOUR SHIFTS.
IN FACT, MARCO IS LEADING A TEAM OVER THERE RIGHT NOW.
...AND IT LOOKS LIKE THEY SHOULD BE BACK ANY MINUTE NOW.
EVERYTHING IS VERY BY THE BOOK, SCHEDULED... NOT AS **EXCITING** AS THINGS WERE IN YOUR DAY... BUT THAT'S HOW WE PREFER IT.
OH, YEAH?

CYNTHIA, LOOK OUT!
AAIIIEEEE!
GOT YOU!

YOU OKAY?
I'M FINE, BUT WE LOST THE WHOLE DAY'S HAUL.
ALL THIS CRAP IS EASILY REPLACED--
WHAT THE HELL WAS THAT?
NO CLUE. THOSE THINGS ARE NOT USUALLY HOSTILE...
DON'T KNOW WHAT COULD HAVE STARTLED THEM.
WHO CARES? THE DAY'S A BUST. LET'S HEAD BACK.
WAIT. DO YOU HEAR--
WHAT IS--

THAT?!

GET OUT OF HERE!
GO!
WHAT ARE YOU GOING TO DO?
DISTRACT THEM--TRY TO BUY YOU TIME!
WHAT ARE YOU DOING?
I'M NOT GOING TO LEAVE YOU ALONE TO FACE THOSE THINGS. WE'VE NEVER SEEN **ANYTHING** LIKE THIS BEFORE.
FWOPP
FWOPP
MY BELT'S NOT WORKING!
AAGH!

I'M NOT LEAVING YOU.
MARCO, DON'T--
TEKK!
DON'T MOVE.
FWAAAASH!
AACK!

HUH?
WHUDD!
OH, GOD!
ST-ST-STAY BACK!

CYNTHIA?!
YOU'RE NOT IN A DESIGNATED TRANSFER ZONE--
WHAT HAPPENED?
THERE WERE--
THERE--
HUFF!
HUFF!
THESE MEN--BUT THEY WEREN'T MEN--
ALIENS-- OH, GOD, THEY WERE ALIENS--
MARCO AND THE REST OF THE TEAM--THEY GOT THEM...
NATHAN--?!
WHAT ARE YOU DOING?!

NATHAN!
NATHAN!
MY GOD-- NATHAN! YOU CAN'T!
THERE'S NO TIME TO ARGUE!
IF I DON'T FIND THEM NOW, I MAY NEVER FIND THEM!
DON'T--IT'S TOO DANGEROUS.
ONCE THEY'RE GONE, THEY'RE GONE--
I CAN'T DO THAT TO MARCO.

WAIT--
DO YOU KNOW WHAT THESE ALIENS ARE?
I HAVE NO IDEA.
FWASH!
OH, GOD...

SAVE YOUR STRENGTH. WE DON'T HAVE TO DO THIS NOW.
NO-- LISTEN TO ME.
THEY HAD THESE FLOATING MACHINES... THEY WERE PULLING OUR PEOPLE INTO THEM. ONE OF THEM HAD ME, BUT I BROKE FREE.
IT WASN'T HURTING US--IT WAS CAPTURING THEM. OUR PEOPLE ARE OUT THERE, ED--
THEY'RE ALIVE.
ED?
ED!
ED, WAIT--
WHAT ARE YOU DOING?

I'M GOING TO FIND THEM.

HEATHER!
HEATHER!
DIRECTOR WARD?
WHERE IS NATHAN?
WHAT DID YOU EXPECT HIM TO DO?
THOSE PEOPLE ARE IN DANGER.
I EXPECT HIM TO FOLLOW THE RULES!
AND DON'T TAKE THAT TONE WITH ME. I'M NOT THE BAD GUY HERE. I'M TRYING TO HELP, SO LET ME MAKE THIS CLEAR--
YOU NEED TO KEEP ME IN THE LOOP ON EVERY SINGLE THING THAT HAPPENS FROM THIS POINT ON. I NEED TO KNOW WHEN HE COMES BACK, I NEED TO KNOW WHAT HE DID WHILE HE WAS OVER THERE, AND NO MATTER WHAT HAPPENS, WE NEED TO KEEP THIS QUIET!
I'M TRYING TO KEEP YOUR BOYFRIEND OUT OF PRISON!

OH, GOD.
KLIK-WIRRRRR!
AHHH!
WHUMP!
OOF!
JILL, IS THAT YOU?
DEREK?
ARE WE ALL HERE? ARE WE ALL ALIVE?
I DON'T KNOW, I CAN'T SEE A DAMN THING. IT'S SO BRIGHT HERE.
WHAT ABOUT DANE? IS HE HERE?
MAYBE HE GOT AWAY.

AGGH!
MOVE.
THAT THING-- IT'S STILL HERE!
IT SOUNDS LIKE THERE'RE MORE OF THEM!
JUST KEEP MOVING FORWARD. YOU WON'T BE HARMED.
GO ON. DON'T BE SCARED.
THERE'S NOTHING TO BE AFRAID OF.
THAT ONE SOUNDS DIFFERENT...
JUST DO WHAT IT SAYS-- I CAN'T GO BACK INTO ONE OF THOSE BALLS.

CRAP!
OUT OF ROOFTOPS.

C'MON!
C'MON!

SCREW IT!

WHUMP!

HURRRRG
AW, CRAP.

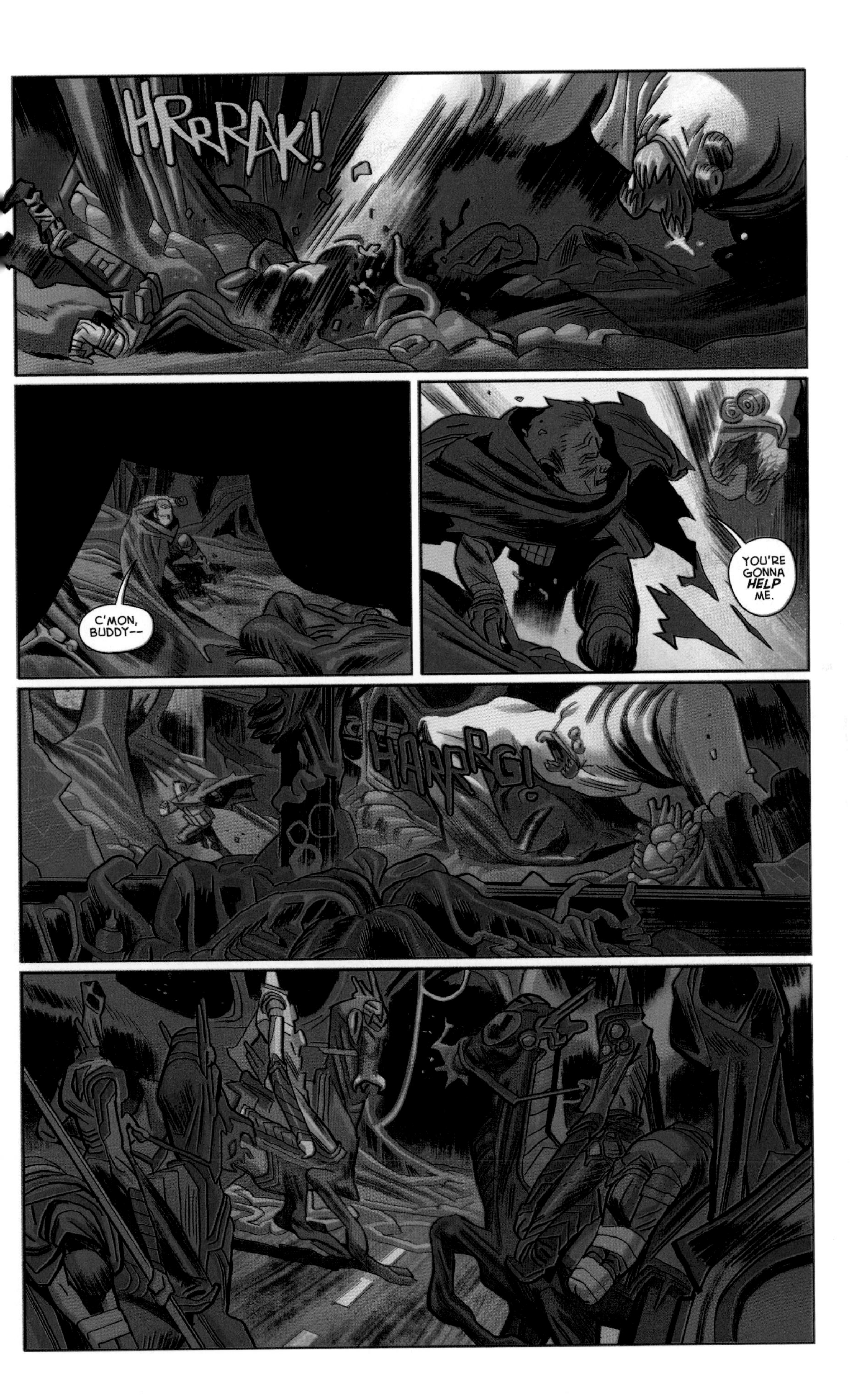
HRRRAK!
C'MON, BUDDY--
YOU'RE GONNA HELP ME.
HARRRG!

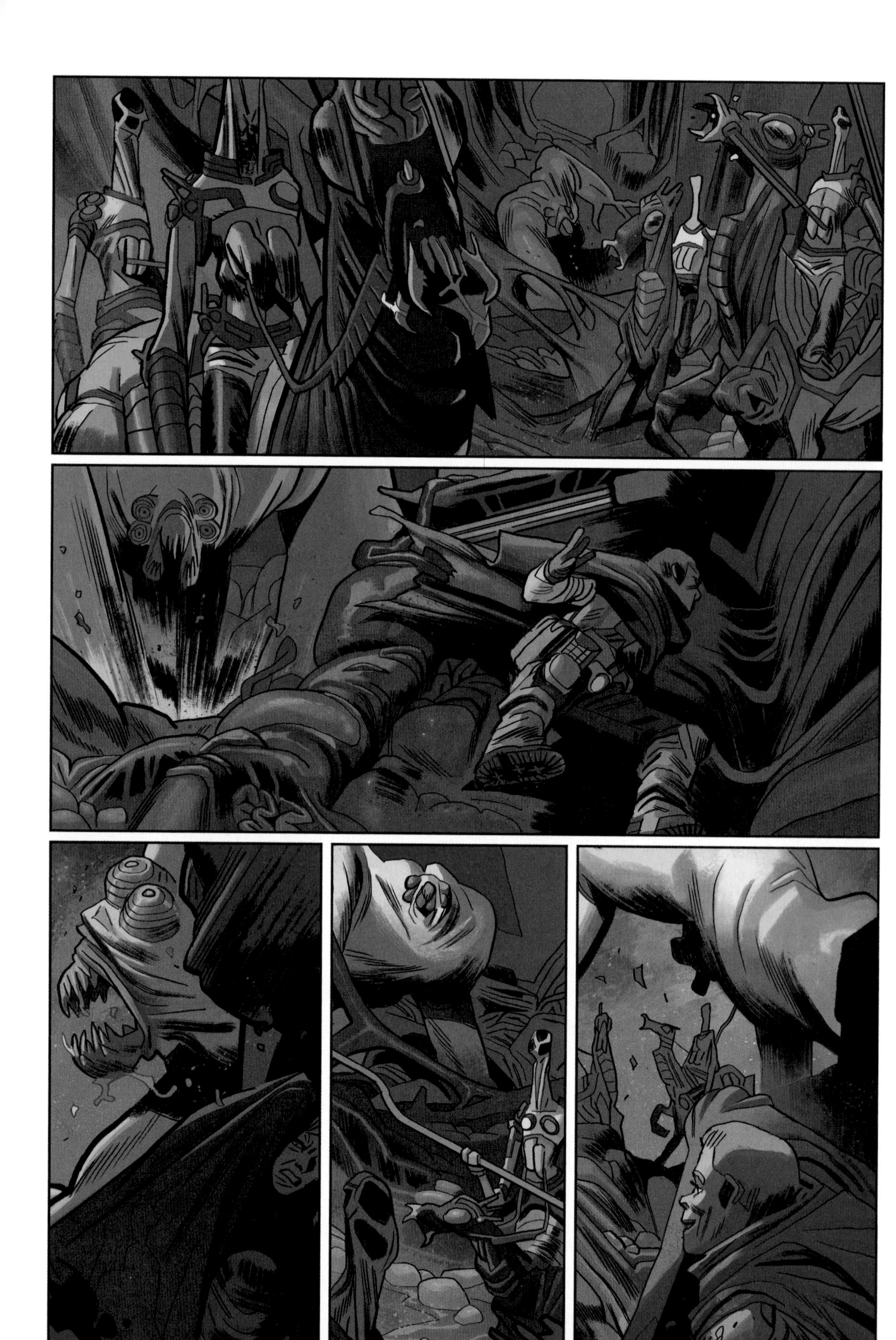

GOTTA EVEN THE ODDS.
FUNT
THREE... TWO...
FUNT
BEEP BEEP
BEEP
FA-FAASH!

FA-FAASH!
HURRAAK!
WRAKK
WROKK

FUNT
BEEP BEEP
FUNT!
FA-FAAASH!
MARCO?
JUST US NOW-- YOU WITH ME?
CAN'T... FEEL LEGS.
LET'S GET YOU HOME.
FA-FAAASH!

C'MON...
C'MON...
WHERE ARE YOU?
HANG IN THERE, GIRL. I KNOW YOU'RE TIRED...
JUST A LITTLE WHILE LONGER.

I'M TELLING YOU, I FEEL FINE.
WHATEVER IT WAS, IT'S WORN OFF.
I'M SORRY, MARCO, BUT YOU WERE EXPOSED TO SOME KIND OF ALIEN SEDATIVE. THIS IS GOING TO REQUIRE MORE THAN A GLANCE.
UH-OH.
WHAT THE HELL WERE YOU THINKING?
I DIDN'T REALLY HAVE TIME TO THINK. THEY WERE ATTACKED. I KNEW IF I HAD ANY CHANCE TO GET THEM BACK, I HAD TO ACT FAST.
IF I'D WAITED, WE PROBABLY NEVER WOULD HAVE FOUND THEM.
I KNOW, I KNOW. IT'S JUST, THERE ARE CLEARANCES NOW, AND WE MONITOR WHO GOES OVER AND WHEN. IT'S ALL LOGGED, IT'S ALL OFFICIAL.
I'M JUST TRYING TO KEEP YOU OUT OF PRISON.
I KNOW.
I APPRECIATE IT.
THOSE THINGS THAT ATTACKED THEM...
WHAT WERE THEY?
I DON'T KNOW.

THRAK-KA-KASH!
V-ZAPP
SKREEEE
HAS TO BE THEM--
SORRY, GIRL--WE GOTTA GO BACK!

FWEE THOO FWAA THEE.
THRAKKK KRAAASH!
WHERE--?
WHERE COULD THEY--?
WHAT'S--

VOMMP!
SKEEERAAC!

WAS THAT A LASER?
WHAT WERE THEY SHOOTING AT?
FWOOM!
STOP!

HE'S NO USE TO US ALONE.
KEEP YOUR DISTANCE. TRACK HIM.
HE'LL LEAD US RIGHT TO THE REST OF MY PEOPLE.

ETERIA
I WOULD HOPE THIS WOULD BE CLEAR AFTER EVERYTHING I'VE DONE, BUT I FEEL THE NEED TO MAKE SURE YOU KNOW...
THAT I'M *NOT* THE BAD GUY HERE.
I BELIEVE THAT NOW, BUT I CAN'T FORGET THAT HASN'T ALWAYS BEEN THE CASE.
IF YOU'RE REFERRING TO MY PLANS FOR YOUR DEVICE, I ASSURE YOU THEY WERE MUCH MORE ALONG THE LINES OF WHAT WE'RE DOING NOW WITH OBLIVION, AND LESS THE FANTASY OF BLASTING ENEMY CITIES INTO AN ALIEN DIMENSION.
IT WAS ALWAYS A ***HUMANITARIAN*** PLAN.

AND YET FOR SOME REASON, I STILL SLEEP EASIER KNOWING MY DEVICE IS OUT OF YOUR HANDS.
FAIR ENOUGH.
BUT THERE'S SOMETHING YOU NEED TO UNDERSTAND ABOUT OUR CURRENT SITUATION HERE.
THERE'S A LOT OF GOOD NEWS COMING OUT OF THIS OPERATION, WORLD CHANGING GOOD NEWS, AND THAT'S WHY IT IS ALLOWED TO CONTINUE.
EVERY LITTLE BREAKTHROUGH, EVERY NEW DISCOVERY, IT BUYS US TIME TO GET US TO THE NEXT ONE. BUT MAKE NO MISTAKE--THAT CLOCK IS ALWAYS TICKING, AND WE'RE ONE PIECE OF BAD NEWS FROM GETTING SHUT DOWN.
THAT IS WHY EVERYTHING IS SO STRICT HERE. EVERY ENTRY AND EXIT OF OBLIVION IS LOGGED AND DOCUMENTED. REPORTS ARE FILED, AND EVERY LITTLE THING IS MONITORED.
NOT BECAUSE I'M A HARD-ASS OR BECAUSE I'M TRYING TO MAKE THINGS DIFFICULT...
IT'S BECAUSE I'M TRYING MY DAMNEDEST TO KEEP THIS PROJECT UP AND RUNNING.

NEW LIFE HAS BEEN DISCOVERED IN OBLIVION, AND IT DOESN'T SEEM TO BE ALL THAT FRIENDLY.
WOULD I BE CORRECT IN ASSUMING A NEW THREAT LIKE THAT SUDDENLY POPPING UP WOULD BE CLASSIFIED AS ***BAD NEWS?***
YOU WOULD.
THEN MAYBE BEFORE THAT'S REPORTED, IT'D BE WISE TO ALLOW ME BACK IN SO THAT I CAN GET MORE ANSWERS, SO THERE'S LESS GUESSWORK INVOLVED WHEN YOU REPORT TO YOUR SUPERIORS.
I DON'T THINK THAT'S WISE.
MY BROTHER IS THERE, AND HE'S GOT A WHOLE CAMP OF PEOPLE WHO ARE VULNERABLE TO THIS NEW THREAT. AT THE VERY LEAST, I HAVE TO ***WARN THEM.***
YOU SAY YOU'RE NOT THE BAD GUY? ***PROVE IT*** AND LET ME ***GO.***

DANE, WHAT ARE YOU DOING?!
BEEN TOO LONG!
HE'S NOT BACK YET, BUT THERE'S NO REASON TO WORRY--DANE! COME BACK!
NO! IF HE'S NOT BACK YET, IT'S BECAUSE THE FACELESS MEN HAVE HIM!
WE HAVE TO DO SOMETHING!

STOP HIM BEFORE HE HURTS HIMSELF!
NO-- STAY BACK!
NO! LET ME GO!
THOSE THINGS HAVE MY PEOPLE! ED IS PROBABLY WITH THEM. THEY'RE ALONE! THEY'RE SCARED!
WE HAVE TO ORGANIZE! WE HAVE TO SAVE THEM BEFORE IT'S TOO LATE!
DANE-- CALM DOWN. I PROMISE WE'RE DOING EVERYTHING WE CAN.
LET'S GET YOU BACK INSIDE SO YOU CAN REST.
NO!
NO!
OH MY GOD...
WHAT--?
WHAT IS--?

OH MY GOD--!
ED!

OH, GOD.
OH, GOD.
WHERE ARE MY CREW?! DID YOU SEE THEM?!
HE'S BARELY BREATHING!
GET HELP!
ED...
WHAT IS GOING ON OUT THERE?

SAVE YOUR STRENGTH. YOU DON'T HAVE TO TALK NOW. IT CAN WAIT.
NO... THIS CAN'T.
SOMETHING IS OUT THERE... IT SHOT ME DOWN.
SILVERWING... **SHE'S DEAD.**
OUR PEOPLE? DID YOU SEE ANY SIGN OF THEM?
NO... BUT I DID SEE THE FACELESS MEN.
THEY'RE REAL.
H--HOW MANY OF THEM?

THERE WERE FOUR OR FIVE OF THEM. THEY WERE RIDING THESE HORSE-LIKE CREATURES. THEY HAD WEAPONS. THEY SHOT AT ME.
BUT THAT'S NOT WHAT ***SHOT*** ME DOWN.
THAT WAS SOMETHING ELSE-- BIGGER. IT WAS DEEPER IN THE JUNGLE.
IT WAS LIKE THEY'D CALLED IN ***BACKUP.***
DEEPER IN THE JUNGLE? DID YOU GET A GOOD LOOK AT THE AREA? COULD YOU FIND IT AGAIN?
YES. THAT COULD BE WHERE THEY'RE KEEPING OUR PEOPLE. COULD HAVE BEEN A BASE OF SOME SORT.
WE NEED TO GATHER A RAIDING PARTY... AND GET OUR PEOPLE BACK.
YOU'RE NOT GOING ***ANYWHERE.*** YOU BARELY MADE IT BACK HERE ALIVE.
LUCY, THESE THINGS HAVE WEAPONS, THEY'RE INTELLIGENT. THEY'RE UNLIKE ***ANYTHING*** WE'VE SEEN HERE BEFORE.
WE DON'T KNOW WHAT THEY'RE PLANNING, BUT WE HAVE TO FIND OUT...
BEFORE IT'S ***TOO LATE.***

THE--
CAAAMP.
WE
FOOOUND
THEMMM.
GOOD
WORK.

PREPARATIONSSS WILL BE MADE.
I'LL BE READY.
I KNOW YOU! YOU'RE KEITH. YOU WERE EXILED WHEN YOUR WIFE AND DAUGHTER DISAPPEARED! YOU SAID THESE THINGS TOOK THEM, BUT NO ONE BELIEVED YOU.
WHY ARE YOU WORKING WITH THEM?! WHAT'S WRONG WITH YOU?!
BEST IF YOU KEEP QUIET.
THEY CAN MUZZLE YOU.
OH, GOD.

HONESTLY, NATHAN, WE'RE LUCKY WARD IS LETTING YOU OFF WITH A WARNING. CAN'T YOU JUST TAKE THE WIN AND MOVE ON?
I'M GLAD YOU SAVED MARCO AND THOSE SCIENTISTS. IT WAS THE RIGHT THING TO DO, BUT IT DOESN'T MAKE IT ANY LESS DANGEROUS.
THERE ARE RULES NOW.
THIS IS A BIG OPERATION, AND THAT COMES WITH OVERSIGHT. YOU REALLY ARE JEOPARDIZING EVERYTHING BRIDGET AND DUNCAN HAVE ACCOMPLISHED BY DOING WHAT YOU DID.
AND NOW THERE ARE NEW CREATURES OVER THERE THAT YOU'VE NEVER ENCOUNTERED? THAT'S INSANE. WARD'S PEOPLE WERE FREAKING OUT. I DON'T KNOW WHEN THEY'LL BE SENDING ANOTHER EXPEDITION OVER... IF EVER.
I KNOW YOU'RE WORRIED ABOUT YOUR BROTHER AND THE REST OF THE PEOPLE IN OBLIVION, BUT THERE'S JUST NOTHING YOU CAN DO.

ED-- NO!
PLEASE DON'T DO THIS!
I'M SORRY, LUCY, I HAVE NO CHOICE.
OUR PEOPLE ARE OUT THERE. WE CAN'T JUST LEAVE THEM. WE HAVE TO DO SOMETHING.
YOU'RE IN NO CONDITION TO GO BACK OUT THERE. NEITHER IS DANE, FOR THAT MATTER.
I SEE WHY YOU THINK YOU HAVE TO DO THIS, BUT YOU CAN'T.
LUCY, I...

QUICKLY!
GET THE BABY *INSIDE!*

LOOK OUT FOR THOSE FLOATING ORBS!
THAT'S WHAT THEY USED TO CAPTURE US!
THEY MAY HAVE BETTER WEAPONS, BUT THEY DON'T KNOW OUR CAMP!
KEEP MOVING! STRIKE WHEN YOU HAVE AN OPENING-- THEN HIDE!
FWAAAPP
ACK!
WUDD
THIS IS TOO MUCH FOR US!
RELEASE THE OGRES!
SIR, WE CAN'T!
THIS IS WHY WE HAVE THEM-- DO IT!

OH, GOD!
OH, GOD!
WRAMM
WRAKOOM
HURRAUGGH!

NO!
NO!
WOMP!
CRUNK!
LUCY!
LUCY!
LUCY.

NO!
WHAP!
UNGGH!

DAMN IT!
AAAHHHHHH!

WRAMM!
NATHAN--?!
GRAB THE ROPE BEFORE I DROP YOU!

OH MY GOD. THIS IS MY FAULT...
I LED THEM HERE.
NO TIME FOR THAT NOW--
WE CAN STILL SAVE THEM!

THEY GOT EVERYONE. THE WHOLE PLACE IS EMPTY...
THERE'S NOTHING WE CAN DO.
NO, THERE'S STILL TIME.
OH, GOD...
THEY GOT LUCY AND SCOTT...
THEY'RE GONE.
WHO'S SCOTT?
MY SON...
YOU NAMED HIM AFTER DAD?
...

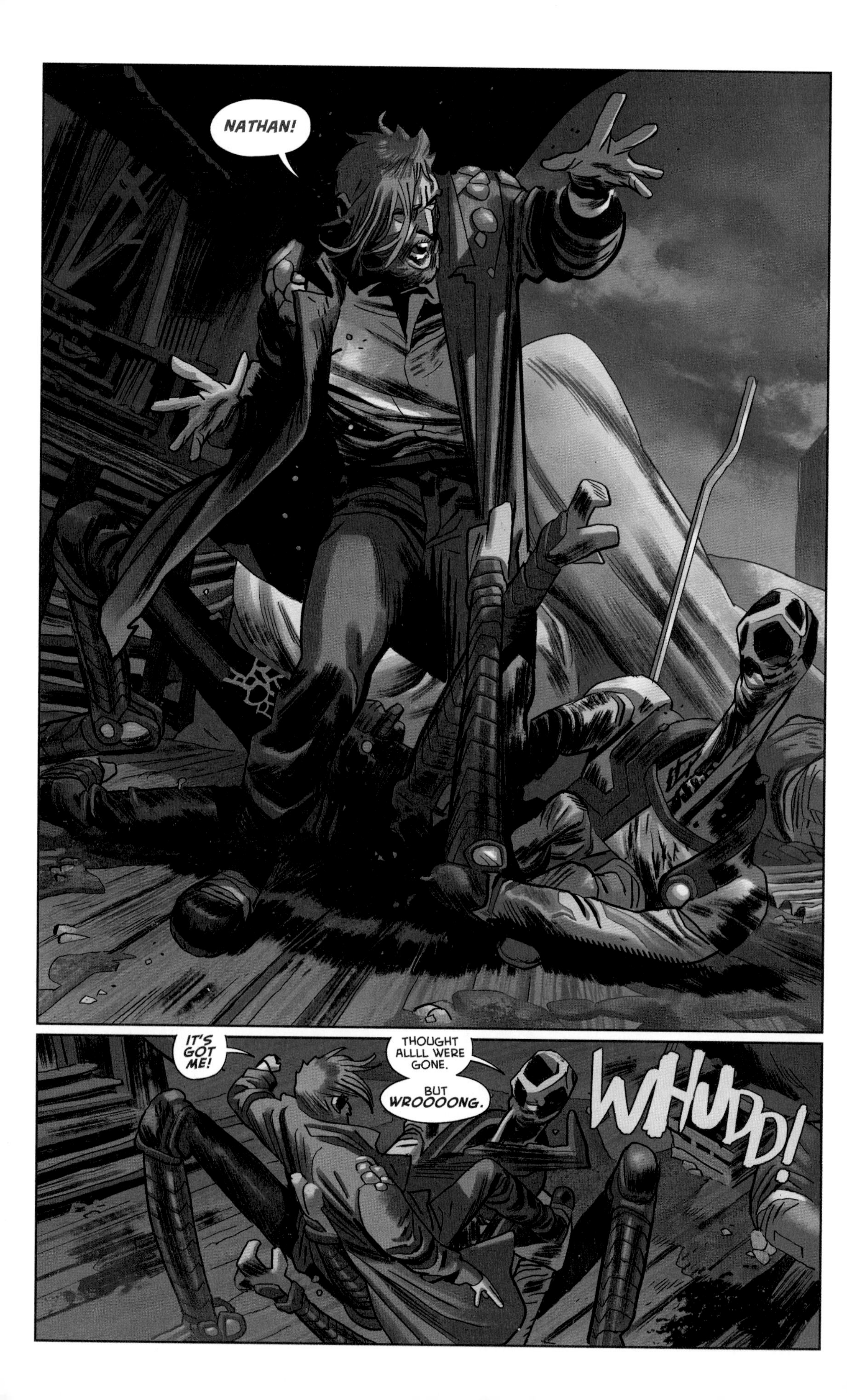
NATHAN!
IT'S GOT ME!
THOUGHT ALLLL WERE GONE.
BUT WROOOONG.
WHUDD!

LET MY BROTHER GO!
BROTHHHER?
WHAT ISSS BROTHHHER?
IF THIS BROTHHHHER-- THISSS MIIINE FOR STUDY.
YOU ARE MIIINE, TOO.
YESSS?

VERY FASSST.
WHAT ARE YOU?
YOUR KIND CALLL US FACELESSSS MEN... BUT WE HAVE FACESSSS.
JUSSST DIFFERENT.
YEAH-- DIFFERENT.
YOU OKAY, ED?
ED?!

DAMN IT.
SHUKK
USUALLY, I'M AGAINST THIS SORT OF THING, BUT YOU'RE **CLEARLY** INTELLIGENT AND OUT TO HURT US, SO I'M MAKING AN EXCEPTION.
WHAT ISSS **EXCEPTIONN?**

SHUKKK!
SHRAAAKK!
NOOO!

NATHAN!
THAT KILL IT?
I'M NOT GOING TO WAIT AROUND TO FIND OUT.
NO, DON'T--!
I KNOW WHAT I'M DOING.
FUNT
BEEP BEEP
LET'S GET YOU BACK.
NO...
WON'T LEAVE YOU.
FWAAAASH!
I'M COMING WITH YOU.
I ALWAYS WEAR THIS.

MHP
BOOSH
FWUMP!
SPLUGG!

OH, GOD...
OH, GOD...
NOT ONE OF MY BEST IDEAS.
DON'T JUST SIT THERE GAWKING-- CALL AN *AMBULANCE!*

HANG IN THERE, LITTLE BROTHER...

Jefferson University Hospital
Jefferson Hospital
SKREEEECH!
HEATHER, WAIT!
EXCUSE ME!
SORRY!
PARDON ME!
WHAT FLOOR IS NATHAN COLE ON?! HE WAS JUST BROUGHT IN WITH A STAB WOUND! I THINK HE'S IN SURGERY!
OKAY, LET ME LOOK HIM UP...
WHAT FLOOR?!

I JUST WANT TO SEE HIM!
MA'AM, YOU CAN'T--

GET HER OUT OF HERE!

THE DOCTORS ARE DOING EVERYTHING THEY CAN. YOU'D JUST BE IN THE WAY.
I KNOW. I'M SORRY.
PLEASE, MA'AM, JUST WAIT HERE WITH THE REST OF YOUR PEOPLE.
THANK YOU.
OH MY GOD. HOW IS HE?
I HAVE NO IDEA.
THERE WAS... SO MUCH BLOOD...
EDWARD COLE?
YEAH?
IF YOU DON'T WANT TO SPEND THE REST OF YOUR LIFE ROTTING IN PRISON--PRETEND YOU'RE NOT HERE.
DON'T LEAVE THIS ROOM. DON'T TALK TO ANYONE. AND FROM THIS POINT ON, ONLY DO WHAT I TELL YOU TO DO.
YEAH, OKAY.
WHATEVER YOU SAY.

OKAY, THEN.
MARIA, I'M--
OH MY GOD. WHAT HAPPENED TO NATHAN?

THESE CREATURES ATTACKED. NATHAN WAS STABBED...
THEY TOOK **EVERYONE.**
LUCY?

...AND OUR BABY BOY.

MARIA, I'M SO SORRY.
YOU DON'T HAVE TO BE. IT WAS A LONG TIME AGO.

WHAT THE--?!
OOF!
WHUDD
YOU CAN WALK IN VOLUNTARILY OR BE CARRIED IN.
I WOULDN'T TRY ANYTHING, DANE.

YOU--!
AW-- NO LOVE FOR YOUR OLD FRIEND KEITH?
YOU'RE BEHIND THIS? HOW COULD YOU TURN ON YOUR PEOPLE LIKE THIS?
MY PEOPLE?
ALL I SEE ARE THE PEOPLE WHO THOUGHT I MURDERED MY OWN FAMILY AND EXILED ME FOR IT.
I WOULDN'T SAY THOSE ARE "MY PEOPLE".
NOW TURN AROUND AND GET BACK IN LINE, OR YOU'RE GOING TO FIND OUT HOW CRUEL MY PEOPLE CAN BE.

Jefferson University Hospital
Jefferson Hospital
REALLY? DROP ME ON A BIG GORILLA MONSTER? THAT WAS YOUR PLAN?
WE CALL THEM OGRES NOW.
WELL, I FOR ONE AM GRATEFUL HE GOT YOU BACK HERE IN ONE PIECE.

I'M SORRY.
IT'S OKAY. THAT MANY PEOPLE TAKEN--HAD TO LEAVE A TRAIL.
WE'LL FIND THEM. I KNOW WE WILL.
NO, I SAW THEM. IT WAS THREE YEARS AGO. I SAW ONE OF THEM, AT LEAST. IT WAS ONLY FOR A SPLIT SECOND. I NEVER TOLD ANYONE BECAUSE I THOUGHT I WAS SEEING THINGS.
AT THE TIME, I COULDN'T REALLY MAKE OUT WHAT I SAW, BUT AFTER WITNESSING THAT ATTACK, IT HAD TO BE ONE OF THEM.
NOT FEELING GUILTY ABOUT NOT SAYING SOMETHING. THIS ISN'T THAT. I DON'T FEEL RESPONSIBLE FOR THE ATTACK ON YOUR COMMUNITY.
I KNOW I COULDN'T HAVE KNOWN THIS WOULD HAPPEN.
WHAT I SAW LOOKED LIKE A BASE. I THINK I KNOW HOW TO FIND THEM.

IT'S OKAY, HONEY. DON'T BE SCARED.

CLEARED FOR EEENTRY. ACCESSS TO ZONE FOUR ONLY.
I'M JUST GOING HOME.

DAD!
YOU'RE BACK!
CAREFUL, KRISSY!
YOU'RE GOING TO KNOCK ME OVER.
OH, KEITH. WHAT DID THEY MAKE YOU DO THIS TIME?
IT DOESN'T MATTER. I'M HERE WITH YOU NOW.